THE SPIRIT
REMAINS

THE SPIRIT REMAINS

Ashley Moyé

No Commission Publishing™

Dee Dee
1978-1987

A puppy's love is pure and true

Custom-made
Just for you.

The old man walked slowly through the cold, December night. His methodic footsteps sank into the white blanket beneath him, crunching through the untraveled pathway. Fluffy snowflakes fell softly around him, as mist from his breath clung to the air. All along the trail, ancient pine trees hung heavily, as blankets of snow and twinkling ice draped their limbs in a somber shroud.

Closely following behind him, panting loudly, was the old man's faithful companion. Chipper was a bit overweight. Well, a lot. But that didn't stop the old boy from keeping up with the old man. No sirree!

Chipper had been with Dan for as long as he could remember. He even remembered the day that he found the old man; sitting on a log, drinking beer with some of the fellows from the pub. At first, the men made fun of Chipper. His coat was pretty scruffy, sure, but his mother wasn't around to clean him up. The rest of the litter was already gone. They just wouldn't wake up.

The old man liked the pup, though, and took him in. Chipper loved the old lady, too. She had fed him with a bottle and dressed him up real cute-like. The old man just roared with laughter when he saw what she did.

The old man doesn't laugh much anymore, though. One day, Chipper found her, just like he found the rest in his litter. She had the same, cold smell to her. Whining, he had gone for the old man, who cried and cried. The old man wouldn't touch Chipper for months after that. Mostly, he just drank.

Eventually, the old man grew accustomed to not having her around and became even closer to Chipper. He didn't go anywhere without him. He spoiled the dog something awful, too. Chipper didn't want for anything.

Nowadays, the old man makes his evening trek out to Earl's Diner for dinner and a few beers. Every night, around six o'clock, the old man and Chipper hike the twenty minutes into town from the cabin, and every night is the same. Worn out from the walk, Chipper plops down beneath Dan's usual table, as Dan eases onto the booth's red vinyl upholstery. Mary comes over with her tray and gives Dan his beer, Coors on tap with a big, frothy white mountain of foam on top.

"Evening, Dan," she says. "How's your back doing?"

Dan just nods his head. "Fine, Mary."

This evening was a bit different, though. Tonight, there were some young punks sitting at the counter. All of them were pretty drunk. The three of them didn't notice the old man and his dog come into the old, converted log cabin, not until Mary walked by with Chipper's water dish. The youngest looking one had been watching the young woman all evening. He was still watching her as she passed him.

"Hey, honey," he said. "What animal of a man drinks his ale from a damn dog bowl?" He stood up and followed Mary over to Dan's table. As he came upon the dog, a look of shock and disgust shadowed his face. "If that don't beat all! Hey, guys. Come take a look at what the cat dragged in. Damn, mister. Ain't ya got no compassion for that poor dog ya got there? Damn thing looks like he's on his last leg there!"

Chipper weakly wagged his tail, as he looked up at the old man. Uncomfortably, Mary set the dish down in front of Chipper. Dan was all red-faced, but continued to fondly pet Chipper on the head.

The young man laughed meanly and turned to his friends. "I bet ya the dog's gonna be stew in this here dump by next week!"

His friends started laughing with him, cackling, and slapping their knees. They abruptly ceased their hysterics, though, when the owner of the diner bellowed from behind the counter, "Hey, buddy. Why don't you just sit your ass down here at the bar and mind your own business, before I come over there and shove your young, little weenie butt out of my restaurant!" Earl glared at the young man, as he returned to his stool, mumbling something to himself.

The incident was soon forgotten by the three punks, and they started having an argument about some girl they knew from the previous town they visited.

Apologetically, Mary returned with Dan's beer. "Don't mind them, Dan. Those guys are drunk. I think Chipper looks just fine. He's going to be around for a long time, still. Don't you worry none." She tried to smile reassuringly, but it was obvious that she didn't believe what she had said.

Dan nodded and looked down at Chipper, who by now was resting his head on his paws, waiting patiently for dinner to be served. Dan knew the truth. He also knew that it wasn't just Chipper who'd be leaving soon. His thoughts were interrupted by Mary.

"Will it be the usual, Dan?" To her surprise, he looked right at her and smiled warmly.

"No, Mary," he replied. "I want your best steak tonight, medium rare. And cut one up for old Chipper here, too."

Mary smiled brightly. "Coming right up!"

❉ ❉ ❉

The wooden floors creaked under the old man's weight, as Dan walked over to the fireplace to put another log on the already blazing fire. Chipper was resting quietly near the hearth on his favorite throw rug. The grandfather clock, standing alone in the corner, was forever accounting for each passing second. Dan looked up at it, just as the hands turned to eleven o'clock. The clock chimed. Dan looked at the dog then, and patted Chipper on the head. The dog opened his eyes, thanking the old man, and returned to sleep.

The old man wearily stood up, shuffled over to his big, overstuffed, easy chair, and lowered himself into a comfortable position. On the end table to his left, a picture of an elderly woman, framed in silver, sat amongst a collection of other framed photographs. Dan looked them over and picked up her picture. With a sullen face, he admired the elderly woman's radiant beauty. Her eyes emanated serenity and love.

A solitary tear slowly found its way down the old man's cheek, as he listened to the tick-tock of the grandfather clock. The old man looked over at Chipper—his last responsibility. Dan's two children were all grown up and had families of their own. They didn't visit anymore. Dan figured they didn't need him. His wife was gone. Her body was buried up on the hill, just below the tree line. Now all the old man had left to care for was the dog. It wouldn't be too much longer, he guessed, as he stared at the crackling fire. He felt a sense of comfort, as he listened to the wind and snow batting against the windowpane. It reminded him that he felt warm and toasty, inside.

The old man's eyes, no longer able to fight back sleep, slowly slid closed, as Chipper's soft breaths and the ticking of the grandfather clock, lulled the old man into slumber.

✿ ✿ ✿

The old man awoke. Chipper was panting happily and banging his tail on the floor, as he nuzzled his master's leg. The old man smiled and scratched Chipper behind the ears. "You're a good boy, Chipper," he said. "Daddy loves ya." He gingerly replaced the photograph of his deceased wife upon the end table and pushed himself up out of the chair. He then went about fixing a delicious breakfast for the two of them.

Dan thought the old dog seemed extra active this morning and looked at him curiously. He watched in amazement as Chipper barked excitedly and ran around the room. The dog jumped up onto a chair, as Dan questioned him humorously, "Chipper, what has gotten into you this morning? You haven't acted like this in a long time!"

Enjoying the dog's enthusiasm, Dan laughed and fed Chipper his breakfast. He stood before the dog, bewildered as Chipper wolfed down his food and raced to the door. Chipper waited expectantly, wagging his tail, and barking at Dan to let him outside. The old man opened the door. Disbelieving his eyes, he watched Chipper tear outside and run after some snow rabbits. After they were gone, the dog frenziedly dug holes into the snow and chased after imaginary prey, or his tail, whatever fancied the dog. It was wonderful to see Chipper act like this again.

Dan took a deep breath of the crystal-clear morning air. The sun was already shining brightly, reflecting off of the ice and snow with an uplifting brilliance. There was a dinghy out on the lake, carrying two fishermen home from an early morning trip. Dan watched them for a long time, as they rowed out of sight.

He stood in the open doorway, appreciating and truly seeing his environment. It had been too long since he had. The sky was pure and blue, decorated with the billowy, cottony mounds of whipped-topping-type clouds that he adored as a young child. This was the perfect home to retire to, he remembered. He watched Chipper once more. The dog was sniffing around the ground, searching for some long-lost bone. Satisfied, Dan then turned and closed the door.

❊ ❊ ❊

That evening at the diner, Chipper still had the same spunk in him as he did earlier in the morning. He ran up to everyone in the place, looking for a pat on the back and even the occasional kiss. Luckily, the punks who had been there the previous night were noticeably absent.

Mary gave Chipper a tight hug, as she spoke to him lovingly. "Oh, Chipper. You are so chipper this evening!"

she said, giggling. "My goodness, Dan, are you giving this dog something?"

Dan watched the old dog with a loving gleam in his eye. "Nope. He's just happy. He knows he's led a good life."

Mary smiled and nodded in agreement. "That's because you're such a good man, Dan," she said, and started clearing away the dishes.

Dan replied to her cheerfully, "Thanks, Mary. Now, how about some of that pecan pie?"

Mary called back to him, as she walked off, "You got it, Hon!"

Dan looked over at Chipper, who was playfully tugging at some little boy's pant's leg, growling, and wagging his tail as the little boy laughed.

❊ ❊ ❊

Dan, exhausted, sat in his easy chair, nursing a glass of whiskey, and smoking a pipe. As Dan quietly watched the fire burning in the fireplace, Chipper sauntered over to him, and laid his head on Dan's lap. Dan looked down at the white-haired face of the black dog. "That's a good boy, Chipper," he said. Chipper climbed up onto Dan's lap, until he was able to touch Dan's face with his nose. By now, the dog could no longer surprise the old man. So, when Chipper licked Dan's rough chin, Dan, in return, gave the dog a tender hug.

The dog lay on Dan's chest for quite a while, as Dan stroked the old dog's back. When the grandfather clock struck midnight, Chipper slid off the old man, and landed onto the floor. Tiredly, he waddled over to his throw rug and laid himself down to sleep. The old man just snored, as the fire, uncared-for, slowly burned out.

❊ ❊ ❊

The old man rested the last stone on top of the others. The grave appeared to be quite small, compared to the one next to it. This was a lovely spot, though, just before the woods, up on the hill. You could see the mountains off in the distance, and much more of the lake from here. Dan placed a white rose in front of the wooden plaque, which simply read, "Chipper." The old man whispered gratefully to his friend, "Thank you, too." He then turned to his wife's grave, and said, "I still love you, Emily. I guess I'll be seeing you soon."

Dan placed a bouquet of red roses near her headstone, after he forcefully wiped away some of the snow, then he stood to leave. As he walked down the hill to the red cabin near the lake, he paused as if to turn and look back, but instead, he jammed his hands into his pockets and continued on.

❊ ❊ ❊

Dana stood at the end of the weatherworn dock on the lake. A warm, spring breeze softly fanned her curly, brown hair, framing her strong, yet innocent face. The sun shined brightly behind her, creating a halo of glowing red and gold. She hugged herself, as she watched the waves wash over the rocks, and recede back into the body of the lake. She was smiling contentedly as her husband and the real estate agent walked down the wooden dock to join her, discussing property values.

She felt so peaceful out here. The city life was definitely getting to her. This would be the perfect getaway for her and John, especially since Sara came into their lives. They needed an environment like this to escape to on the weekends and vacations.

John was being very businesslike, as usual, always trying to get the better deal. He was pointing out all of the drawbacks to the property, fishing to get a lower price. Dana's eyes were sparkling as she listened to him, doing her best not to laugh. Finally, Julia, the "money grubbing" agent, turned to Dana. "Well, what do you think, Dana? I'll bet you're picturing you and your family having the time of your lives out on that beautiful lake!" she said.

Dana looked at John with amusement. He had a stern expression on his face, warning her not to blow it. She looked the agent straight in the eye, and just said flatly, "I can't swim. In fact, I hate being in the water." She walked passed the two and headed for the red cabin, anxious to see what the adorable, little home looked like on the inside.

John was quite pleased and acted upon Dana's initiative, as he followed her with the agent. "Why don't you tell me straight out. What is it going to cost to fix up this old cabin, Julia?"

Dana excitedly explored the cabin, rushing from room to room. Whenever Julia was around, she did her best to contain herself, but John was still a bit nervous with her expressions of enthusiasm. When Julia excused herself to make a phone call downstairs, John took Dana aside, suppressing his laughter and her squeals of delight.

"Shhh!" he said whispering, as he placed the tips of his fingers over her lips, "Dana, you have got to calm down. I've already knocked $5,000.00 off the asking price, and I think —" but Dana pulled his hand away from her mouth.

"John, this place is perfect! Stop being such a fuddy-duddy and let me enjoy myself!"

They both laughed quietly, knowing that no matter what the price, this cabin would soon be theirs. They looked at each other with the same fire that was there when they first met. Even after Sara was born, when other couples may let the marriage go, theirs was even stronger. John mouthed, "I love you," as he touched her cheek softly. He still made her melt inside when he did that. Dana closed her eyes as John leaned down and gently kissed her lips. With their hearts beating warmly, they looked deeply into each other's eyes as they slowly drew away from one another. Just then, they heard Julia's approaching footsteps, as she rushed up the stairs.

John took Dana's hand, their faces still blushing, and they met Julia at the top of the staircase. Excitedly, Julia announced, "The deceased's son has decided to accept—" but Dana, her face beaming, wouldn't let Julia finish.

"We'll take it!"

✷ ✷ ✷

A small group of snowshoe hares, their summer coats now a rusty brown, warily fed on the greenery just at the edge of the woods, until a child's peals of laughter sent them running for cover.

Little Sara was screaming with delight as the little puppy chased her around the yard. "C'mere, Doodles! Catch me, Doodles, catch me!"

Dana was getting lunch ready on the picnic table and laughed as she watched the puppy topple over, yipping out to Sara.

John and two men were unloading the moving truck, listening to loud rock music, and singing along. Dana turned to watch John screech out a solo, as one of his buddies danced around and tossed boxes to the other. John suddenly noticed her watching. Half-embarrassed, he coughed as he abruptly ended the note. Smiling at Dana, he wiped the sweat from his brow, then waved to her shyly. Dana waved back to him cheerfully and turned again to watch Sara and the puppy run up towards the woods. Worried, she called out, "Sara, don't go too far! Lunch is almost ready!"

The child changed direction, laughing joyously, and ran passed three mounds just below the tree line on the hill. John ran up and joined Dana excitedly. He stood behind her, wrapping his arms around her waist, and hugged her tightly against his chest. Dana smiled broadly and locked her fingers into his, while he reassured her. "Don't worry. Sara's a tough kid," he said. Playfully, he nuzzled her neck with his chin, making her giggle.

Dana twisted around to look up into his glittering eyes. She kissed him sweetly on his cheek, then enthusiastically turned forward again to watch the puppy playfully tugging at Sara's skirt, growling, and wagging his tail, as the little girl laughed.

John looked up then to watch. Both Dana and he smiled happily at the sight. He then tenderly placed his left hand on Dana's swollen abdomen and whispered, "I love you," into her ear. Spasms of delightful chills echoed down her spine. Dana placed her hands on top of his, caressing his velvety skin affectionately. Her eyes watered as she continued to watch the young girl and puppy play.

Suddenly, a flutter of white butterflies caught Dana's attention. Her gaze followed the two clusters, as they circled above Sara and the puppy. They continued their flight over the flowers and raced up the hill, passing over the three graves, through the trees, and then soared up into the sky.

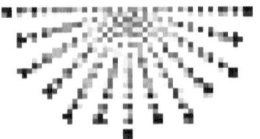

ABOUT THE AUTHOR

Ashley Moyé

After serving as a deputized FBI agent for over 10 years, Ms. Moyé became an adult learner and resumed her college education. Being an ardent advocate of oral health, she earned an A.S. in business administration, while pursuing a bachelor's degree in dental hygiene. As a complement to the upcoming release of Oropris, she is aiming to earn a master's degree in the field of oral health. For more about the author, visit ashleymoye.com.

AUTHOR'S NOTE

The Story Behind The Story

I wrote the first draft of *The Spirit Remains* in 1991. By 1993, thinking that it would make a great short film, to segue into screenwriting, I rewrote the story into a screenplay. So, while working as an extra on *Major League II*, I gave a copy of the screenplay to an acquaintance, hoping to recruit him as a producer for the project.

"J.B.J." worked for a casting company in Baltimore, Maryland. I got the impression that he had local connections, and could probably make things happen. I thought he was a nice guy, and I wanted to work with him. Besides, I thought he was cute. A week or so later, I asked him what he thought of the script. He told me that he didn't think it would go anywhere, and gave it back to me.

Okay. Wasn't his cup of tea, I figured. But, unfortunately, his opinion still resulted in my putting *The Spirit Remains* way far down on my list of priorities.

Flash forward to the set of *The Replacements* in 1999, which starred Keanu Reeves. I was well-thought-of by the extras casting assistant coordinator, who had become well-acquainted with me from prior projects, so she placed me on the football field as a photographer extra (and in the same craft services room as the stars). In short, Keanu eventually informed me that J.B.J. had stolen my script. You see, people within networks **do** talk.

It turned out that J.B.J. had placed his name on the title page as the writer, changed my script's title to *The Family Remains*, then submitted it to his professor at Towson University, as his writing assignment. I guess he had been too busy working on *Major League II*, to do his homework. Well, his professor was so impressed by the script that he made a few calls on his "extraordinarily talented" student's behalf.

The Family Remains eventually was produced into a short film, was entered into a film festival's competition, and won best writer of a short. Then, J.B.J. got hired as a writer by Francis Ford Coppola.

Besides from being dishonest, the biggest mistake that J.B.J. made was arrogantly presuming that I was a nobody, who would never amount to anything, and would never know anybody important. What J.B.J. didn't know was that the very first person who read *The Spirit Remains* was Johnny Depp. In fact, Johnny read the first draft, within days after I completed it, when he stopped by to visit me at my father's house in Springtown, Pennsylvania.

Of course, most people know that Johnny is well-acquainted with Francis. And, most people should know that truths eventually do come out.

After learning of J.B.J.'s act of plagiarism, Francis fired J.B.J., then sounded the alarm. J.B.J. was stripped of his award, and his professor (presumably) cursed J.B.J.'s name. Back when all this happened, though, no one was able to contact me.

J.B.J. has yet to author anything for Hollywood, and, based upon his online résumé, it looks to me like he may be putting parties together as an event planner.

Although it took a while for the betrayal to really sink in with me, I had been so soured by being plagiarized, it has taken me a long time to bring *The Spirit Remains* out again.

Yup. About 20 years.

ALSO BY THIS AUTHOR

WHAT YOUR
EMPLOYEES
CAN'T OR
WON'T TELL
YOU

A handbook for C-suite executives on
how to improve employee retention.

Ashley Moyé

Hardback ISBN 9781734723441
Paperback ISBN 9781734723458
Ebook ISBN 9781734723465

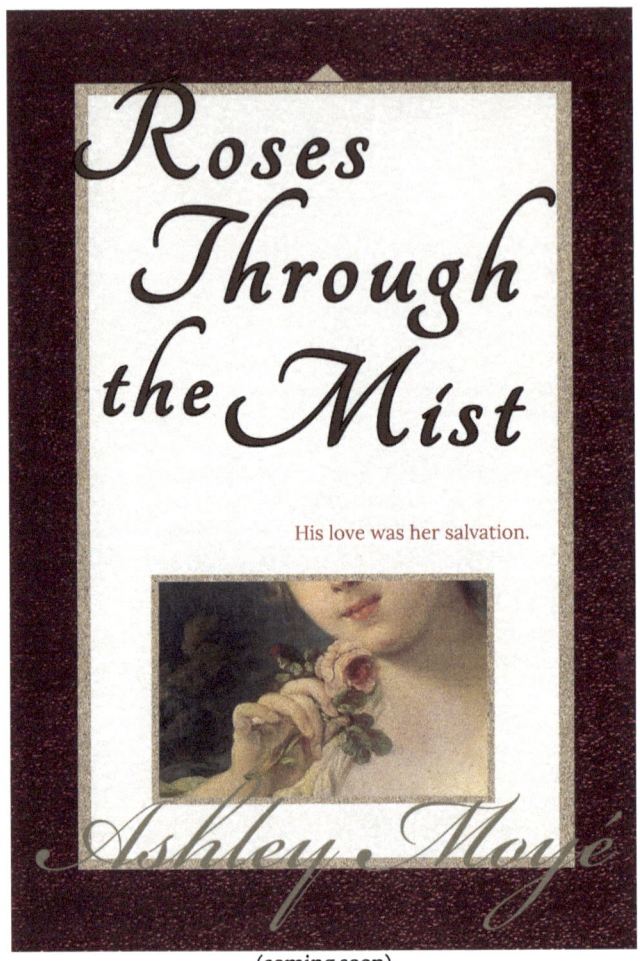

Roses
Through
the Mist

His love was her salvation.

Ashley. Moyé

(coming soon)

ISBN 9781734723427
Ebook ISBN 9781734723410

Sneak Peek....

✽ ✽ ✽

It was a beautiful spring morning. The sky was a clear blue, and clouds edged with a spectrum of colors soared by. Nestling missel thrushes cried demandingly to their parents in a nearby tree. Its leaves waved gently, as a cool breeze caressed its foliage. The flowers were just starting to open. A new day. A new beginning for the world.

Just as the sun was spreading her glowing smile fully upon the land, shining its love over all living things, Victoria opened her lustrous green eyes. It was these eyes that held the potential to melt a man's heart from its icy coldness to the burning waters of desire; however, Victoria had yet to learn of it. She had only recently become of age, and was unlearned in the ways of men.

Eager to face a new day, Victoria arose from her bed and bounded to her dressing table. As she brushed her luxuriously long, fine auburn hair, Victoria began to think of how fortunate she was to have been found by Martin. The doctor had taken her away from the cruelties of poverty, and brought her to the luxuriousness of wealth. She would forever be grateful to him. He was her savior; her guardian angel. She would do anything for him, as he would for her.

Her only wish was that he would spend more time with her. She hadn't even learned what discipline of medical expertise he practiced. For the rare moments they had shared together, he never told her. How strange, she thought. Every time she approached the matter, either something happened or he somehow changed the subject.

Little did she know what his true intentions were. Of the three weeks she had been under his guardianship, Victoria had only witnessed Martin's nicer side, which even then was but a mask.

There was a soft rapping at her bedchamber's door. "Mistress Victoria, I've your breakfast here," Liza squeaked.

Victoria opened the door for the private maid that Martin had hired specifically for her. "Thank you, Liza," she said, greeting Liza with a warm smile.

As always, Liza's chubby face brightened to see such beauty. For her, it was a great honor to have a mistress of such fine quality, although she was a bit dismayed that the young lady had not acquired her negligée, as of yet. Liza thought that Victoria ought to be a bit more modest with her femininity, as she set the tray on the bed. "The doctor requests you to join him in his study after breakfast. Shall I prepare a bath for you, while you enjoy your meal?"

"I would be grateful," Victoria said, as she sat next to the tray. "Might there be rose beads for the water? I believe Martin appreciates it when I make use of them."

"As you wish, miss." Liza took the peach negligée out of the wardrobe and laid it aside of Victoria, then bustled away to the connected lavatory to empty the close stool.

Meanwhile, famished, Victoria happily attacked her morning meal. The Chelsea bun was especially tasty this morning, and the lemon punch was a delightful new treat.

Liza hummed to herself as she went about the arduous chore of preparing Victoria's therapeutic bath in a copper tub. Although the bathing tub had a backrest to one end, to Liza it appeared to be more of a horse trough. For one to sit in a horse trough, surrounded by water, was a strange notion to her, to be sure, but the doctor had insisted that his patient be bathed daily; not unlike Queen Caroline's bathing habits, during her tenure. He was a staunch proponent of Dr. Hahn's medicinal approach, though he did disagree with the sole use of cold water.

It was quite a daunting task for Liza to haul the pails of heated water, from a cauldron in the kitchen, up to the third floor; ergo, she was mindful as to not fill the tub with an excessive amount of water, as she would have to empty it once Victoria was finished.

With a sigh of relief, she poured the last pail of water into the tub's basin, then wiped the sweat from her brow.

"All is ready, miss," announced Liza, as she re-entered Victoria's bedchamber.

"Thank you, Liza. You are such a dear." Victoria finished the last drop of lemon punch, as Liza removed two gowns from Victoria's wardrobe.

"Which gown do you wish for me to ready for you?" Liza said, while holding both gowns up for Victoria.

"I think the one of pink and green would be nice. Do you agree?"

"A perfect choice, miss," she said, returning the other dress to the wardrobe. "You look absolutely divine in that one. You take your bath now. I added the rose beads, just as you wished." With that, Liza took the pink and green gown with her, and quietly shut the door behind her.

Victoria undressed and stepped into the warm water. She leaned back against the tub, and with a heavy sigh of content, closed her eyes....

...She was walking along a stone path through a rose garden. It was utterly breathtaking. There were red, yellow, pink and white roses everywhere she looked. In the center of the garden, stood a white marble statue. Intrigued, Victoria drew closer to see of what it was. She discovered that it was of a woman that looked strikingly similar to her. She had long, flowing curls of hair, like Victoria's. She also had big eyes, a slender nose, a dainty chin and high cheekbones, just like Victoria's. Then, Victoria realized, it was her.

Victoria then heard a man laughing eerily from somewhere within the garden. She looked about herself, but could not tell from which direction it came. She then saw, to her horror, a heavy mist slowly creeping over the roses. Its thickness was seemingly impenetrable of light. It came closer and closer to her, as the man's laughter grew louder. A shiver of fear crawled up her spine. Quickly, Victoria turned back towards the statue and saw that it had started to crumble. Someone was calling her name....

"Victoria, Mistress Victoria," Liza worriedly repeated. "Please, hurry now. The doctor is expecting you!"

"Martin?" Victoria said hazily, then remembering where she was, "Yes, I will Liza. Tell him I shall be with him shortly."

"Yes, miss."

Splashing cold water upon her face, Victoria quickly came back to reality and forgot her strange dream.

Liza picked up the tray of dishes as she hurriedly withdrew from Victoria's bedchamber. Yet, in her haste, she absentmindedly left the door open.

Victoria wrapped a toweling around herself, as she stepped out of the bathing tub, then went to her wardrobe to dress. As she admired her youthful figure in the full-length mirror, a burning feeling crept over her, as though someone was watching her.

And indeed she was correct. Jeffrey Bates stood in the open doorway, as his powerful blue eyes took in the dove before him. Dressed in navy breeches and a red waistcoat, his slim, muscular frame filled the doorway.

Feeling her face grow warm, Victoria slowly turned her head towards the open door, where she saw, to her astonishment, the considerably attractive young man.

As their gaze met, Jeffrey's lips parted as a breath of surprise lifted his broad chest.

Victoria's heart trembled, clutching her breath along with it. Titillating bolts of delight exploded all around her. She could hear the deafening sound of her heart thumping against her chest. As they both stood silently, staring at one another, tiny butterflies flew down Victoria's throat and found their way to her stomach.

Jeffrey appeared as if he might be looking upon a ghost, for his face was draining of all color. Even his thick, flaxen hair seemed to turn paler.

Victoria finally gathered her senses and quickly grabbed her negligée from the bed to conceal her body. "How dare you enter my bedchamber without my permission," she whispered, with a feigned hint of anger.

Jeffrey's eyes widened with anguish, then he quickly turned and disappeared down the hall.

Still clutching her negligée, Victoria rushed to the door and gently closed it. In great distress, she picked up the shift and began to dress herself — a cumbersome chore made infinitely easier upon Liza's return. As Liza deftly braided Victoria's hair and fashioned it into a crown, Victoria sat quietly, the whole while thinking about the strange man. He certainly was not a servant; his clothes were too fine and expensive. Most puzzling of all was her reaction to his presence. She didn't quite understand how a man could make her feel the way he had. That had never happened to her before. Another thought came to her, should she mention this to Martin? Not knowing exactly why, she decided that it would be best not to.

After all was in order and her hair in proper place, Victoria rushed to Martin's study.

Martin was intently examining some papers when Victoria walked in. "Here is my lovely rose," exclaimed Martin, tossing her a devilish grin. He threw his arms around her, then smothered little kisses all over her face. "It is a beautiful morning, isn't it?"

"Quite so." Victoria looked up into his dark hazel eyes. Martin was quite different from that other man, she thought. They were practically opposites.

"What is wrong, my precious rose? You seem so distant."

"Nothing to be concerned of. Shall we be doing anything special today?" With the air of innocence, Victoria smoothed back a loose strand of his thin brown hair, which he had pulled back into a pigtail.

"Well," Martin said, as he broke away, "I have a meeting with this fellow today. It shall very likely consume my entire afternoon." He paused as he pulled a large book from the shelf and started thumbing through its pages. "I expect things shall be quite boring for you all by your lonesome, so I've scheduled you to meet with a dressmaker in the City. I'm sure you'll enjoy yourself, picking out fabrics and patterns and such." He looked at Victoria and smiled. "The carriage should be arriving shortly to take you." He set the book down and took Victoria's arm. "Come, I'll wait with you in the parlor."

Before Victoria could say anything, they were out the door, and down the stairway to the foyer. Victoria felt like she was being dismissed, rather than disported. Before she could voice her opinion, though, Jeffrey appeared at the bottom of the stairwell and came towards them. He was carrying a cup of tea, and smiling broadly. Feeling the butterflies return once more, Victoria willed them to be gone. "Calm yourself," she repeated in her mind.

"Jeffrey," exclaimed Martin with surprise, "I was wondering what had become of you." The three paused on the stairwell.

"I was thirsty and fetched myself some tea. Thank you for offering."

Martin ignored this and continued icily, "Please return to my study. I shall be with you shortly."

"Certainly, Martin. Firstly, you must introduce me to this lovely lady you are escorting." Jeffrey flashed a brilliant smile at Victoria, who was still in shock. She was surprised to see that he acted so coolly after their first confrontation.

"Of course, I beg your pardon," Martin said sarcastically. "Victoria, this is Mr. Bates. Mr. Bates, Victoria."

"'Tis a pleasure to meet your acquaintance, Mr. Bates." Victoria extended her right hand, as the fingers of her left dug into the banister for dear life.

"Indeed, the pleasure is all mine," replied Jeffrey, taking her hand and softly kissing it, "but of course, you may call me Jeffrey, should you find that to your pleasure."

"Thank you," she responded, her heart pounding in her ears.

"Victoria," he said quietly, "an inspiring name to complement your exquisite beauty."

Martin sounded impatient as he rudely broke in, "And Victoria was just leaving." He started down the stairs, leading Victoria along with him. "I do believe your carriage is already here, my darling rose. You wouldn't want to be late for your appointment. I shall see you at dinner." He kissed Victoria on the cheek, as the butler helped her with her overcoat. Martin then turned and started up the stairs.

"I've enjoyed our meeting, Victoria. I hope we shall meet again," Jeffrey called out from the stairwell.

"Thank you, Mr. Bates. I have enjoyed it as well. Farewell, Martin." Victoria turned and stepped outside, hearing the door close behind her.